This book belongs to:

Raif Jamil-altaji

Dear Raif
Happy New Year

Daddu x
Jan 2017

Contents

Cover illustration by Guy Parker-Rees
Text pages 15–18 by Judith Nicholls (© MCMXCVII)

A catalogue record for this book is available
from the British Library

Published by Ladybird Books Ltd
A subsidiary of the Penguin Group
A Pearson Company
© LADYBIRD BOOKS LTD MCMXCVII–

LADYBIRD and the device of a Ladybird are trademarks of
Ladybird Books Ltd Loughborough Leicestershire UK

A quiet night out

written by Geraldine Taylor

illustrated by Guy Parker-Rees

Kim and her family were camping.
That night, Kim and her dad couldn't sleep.
Mum was snoring!

Kim and Dad got dressed and went outside.

"What was that?"
whispered Kim.
"Don't worry," said Dad.
"It's only an owl."

"What was that?" asked Kim.
Dad said, "Don't worry.
It's only a dog."

Kim and her dad nearly fell
over in surprise.
"What was that?" asked Dad.

Tyrannosaurus rex

written by Judith Nicholls

illustrated by Andy DaVolls

I am the **biggest** dinosaur.
My neck is as tall as a tree.
I am **Tyrannosaurus rex**.
Don't touch **me**!

I am the **biggest** dinosaur.
My body's as big as a lorry.
I am **Tyrannosaurus rex**.
If you touch me you'll be **sorry**.

I am the **biggest** dinosaur.
My tail is as strong as a train.
I am **Tyrannosaurus rex**.
I am the **King** of the Plain.

The last dinosaur

written by Marie Birkinshaw
illustrated by Rosslyn Moran

Sam Brown's bedroom was full of dinosaurs. It was also very untidy.

Sam Brown loved collecting
things about dinosaurs,
but he never had time
to put them away.

Now Sam was collecting dinosaur cards, and he needed just one more card for a full set.

The card he needed was
a Giganotosaurus, one of
the last dinosaurs ever
to be found.

He had asked all his friends
at school, but nobody had
the Giganotosaurus.

He asked his mum if he could
go out to get some more
cards. But Mum said no.
She said he had to tidy up
his bedroom.

Sam didn't want to.
Tidying up was really boring.

But then Sam began to like
it. He found some dinosaurs
that he hadn't looked at
for a long time.

Suddenly he saw something
under his bed.
It was a pack of dinosaur cards
that he hadn't opened.
Sam quickly looked inside.
There was a Stegosaurus,
an Apatosaurus and...
a GIGANOTOSAURUS!

At last! Sam had the full set.
Tidying up wasn't so bad,
after all.

Dinosaur Facts

- We know of about 250 different kinds of dinosaurs. There are probably hundreds of different types that have yet to be discovered.

- Dinosaurs existed for 160 million years – a long time compared with the mere two million years or so that humans have been on Earth.

- Tyrannosaurus rex existed 70 million years ago. It was once thought to be the biggest meat-eating dinosaur. Recent discoveries have unearthed an older dinosaur that dwarfed Tyrannosaurus rex. The Giganotosaurus existed 100 million years ago. It weighed between six and eight tonnes and measured 12.5 metres long. It had a huge head, massive jaws and lots of sharp teeth.

- Dinosaurs were probably brightly coloured. Even the drab dinosaurs may have had bright frills and crests.

- The biggest dinosaurs were the long-necked plant-eaters. The biggest was Seismosaurus. It must have weighed 100 tonnes – equal to fifteen elephants.

- The biggest dinosaur footprints discovered so far are over one metre in diameter. They were found in Argentina, in South America.

- The meat-eating dinosaurs used to prey on the plant-eating dinosaurs. So the plant-eaters needed plenty of armour to defend themselves. Some developed spines on their backs and sides and even had clubs on their tails.

- One of the biggest plated dinosaurs was the Stegosaurus. It was seven metres long and lived in North America.

my funny bone's not funny

written by Geraldine Taylor

illustrated by Tania Hurt-Newton

My funny bone's
not funny.
And my big toe's
much too big.

My knees are
wobbly knobbly.
And my leg looks
like a twig.

I wish I could run faster.
I wish I could climb a tree.

I wish I could be lots of things.
But I'm really glad I'm **me!**

The last dinosaur

Still on the dinosaur theme! Help your child's confidence and fluency by gently (and quietly) prompting her with any words she finds tricky. Show her how to break down the long dinosaur names into more manageable bits, for example, A-pat-o-sau-rus. Perhaps she would like to read the story to you again tomorrow or even later today!

She can enjoy listening while it's your turn to read the Dinosaur Facts to her!

My funny bone's not funny

Can your child work out any new words in this rhyme for herself? Offer to help her if she needs it and then have lots of fun listening to her read the rhyme back to you. You could read it together. Has she ever knocked her funny bone? Was it funny?

New words

Encourage your child to use some of these new words to help her to write her own very simple stories and rhymes. Go back to look at earlier books and their wordlists to practise other words.

Read with Ladybird...

is specially designed to help your child learn to read. It will complement all the methods used in schools.

Parents took part in extensive research to ensure that **Read with Ladybird** would help your child to:

- take the first steps in reading
- improve early reading progress
- gain confidence in new-found abilities.

The research highlighted that the most important qualities in helping children to read were that:

- books should be fun – children have enough 'hard work' at school
- books should be colourful and exciting
- stories should be up to date and about everyday experiences
- repetition and rhyme are especially important in boosting a child's reading ability.

The stories and rhymes introduce the 100 words most frequently used in reading and writing.

These 100 key words actually make up half the words we use in speech and reading.

The three levels of **Read with Ladybird** consist of 22 books, taking your child from two words per page to 600-word stories.

Read with Ladybird will help your child to master the basic reading skills so vital in everyday life.

Ladybird have successfully published reading schemes and programmes for the last 50 years. Using this experience and the latest research, **Read with Ladybird** has been produced to give all children the head start they deserve.